MW00914909

Splash medics

30141 Antelope Rd. D-221

Menifee, CA 92584

Printed in the United States of America

First Printing,: March 2016

ISBN: 978-1-48356-651-1

TOBY THE DOLPHIN
AND
WATER SAFETY

Written by Lisa La Russo

Illustrated by Hannah McMillin

Today Ashley and her family decided to visit the dolphins at the Aquarium, but Ashley wasn't very happy.

Toby the dolphin saw Ashley by the
side of the pool and swam over to her.

"What's your name," Toby asked,
"and why are you sad?"

"My Name is Ashley. I want to go in the water and play with you and your friends, but I can't," she said sadly.
"I don't know how to swim."

"Oh I see," said Toby

"You shouldn't swim with us until you learn how
to be safe in the water," Toby said with concern

"But I want to swim with you and all
the other dolphins." Ashley said sadly.
She thought she would never be allowed
to play with Toby.

Toby nudged Ashley with his nose,
"Don't be sad, Ashley,
you just need swimming lessons and to learn the
Water Safety rules. Then you can play with us."

WATER SAFETY RULES
1. Wear a life vest
2. Learn to swim
3. Have a swimming buddy
4. An adult must be watching

"Do you want to learn the water safety song before you go?"

"Sure!" Ashley agreed happily

WATER SAFETY SONG

 Sing to the tune "Row, Row, Row Your Boat"

SWIM SWIM LEARN TO SWIM

KNOW THE SAFETY RULES

WEAR YOUR VEST AND LEARN THE REST

AND YOU'LL BE SAFE IN POOLS

(REPEAT)

"I love your song, Toby!" Ashley said, "I'll get
swimming lessons and learn the rules. Then I can
go swimming with you next time I visit,
I PROMISE!"

Ashley went home and worked hard on her swimming lessons and learned the water safety rules.

WATER SAFETY PLEDGE

1. I WILL LEARN TO SWIM.

2. I WILL USE A SAFETY VEST.

3. I WILL SWIM WITH A BUDDY.

4. I WILL ALWAYS HAVE AN ADULT WATCH ME IN WATER.

5. I PROMISE TO FOLLOW THE WATER SAFETY RULES

Toby watched for her each day. He wondered
if she kept her promise to learn the
water safety rules and if she would come
back to play with him and his friends.

Then one morning, Toby saw Ashley with her family.

"Ashley!"
Toby yelled as he swam towards her

"Toby!" Ashley waved.

"Toby, I learned the water safety rules and I learned how to swim!"

Toby was so happy he did a flip!

"I'm so proud of you, Ashley," Toby smiled. "Before you get into the water let's go over the water safety rules…"

Water Safety Rules

"Number one: I have a life vest

Number two: I know how to swim

Number three: I have my swimming
Buddy, YOU!"

"And what is the last rule?"
Toby asked excitedly

Ashley giggled,
"And number four:
I have an adult
watching me!"

"Great job, Ashley!" Toby said, "Now you can finally swim and play in the pool with me."

"Yay!" Ashley cried happily, as she jumped into the pool with Toby.

"Toby," Ashley said, as they splashed and played, "let's sing the water safety song again!'

"Okay, let's do it, Ashley!" Toby said.

WATER SAFETY SONG

Swim, swim, learn to swim
Know the safety rules
Wear your vest and learn the rest
And you'll be safe in pools

(Repeat)

"Get on my back, Ashley!"
Toby said, "and I'll take you for a ride!"

Ashley hugged Toby tightly as they
sang and swam all around the pool.

WATER SAFETY RULES

1. WEAR A LIFE VEST

2. LEARN TO SWIM

3. HAVE A SWIMMING BUDDY

4. AN ADULT MUST BE WATCHING

DEDICATION

This book is dedicated to all of the children who have been injured or have lost their lives, and to the families who have suffered a loss because of submersion related incidents. Your loss is not forgotten, and your hearts are always with us.

A SPECIAL THANK YOU

to our Sponsors!

A list is available on our website

www.splashmedics.org